For my grandmother, who has always been there for me

Copyright © 2019 by Sang-Keun Kim · Translation copyright © 2019 by Chi-Young Kim
All rights reserved. Published in the United States by Schwartz & Wade Books, an imprint of Random House Children's Books,
a division of Penguin Random House LLC, New York. Originally published in South Korea by Sakyejul in 2017.
Schwartz & Wade Books and the colophon are trademarks of Penguin Random House LLC.
Visit us on the Web! rhcbooks.com
Educators and librarians, for a variety of teaching tools, visit us at RHTeachersLibrarians.com

Library of Congress Cataloging-in-Publication Data is available upon request.
ISBN 978-0-525-58134-5 (hc) — ISBN 978-0-525-58135-2 (glb) — ISBN 978-0-525-58136-9 (ebook)

The text of this book is set in Belen.
The illustrations were rendered in colored pencil, pastel, pen, and compiled digitally.
Book design by Rachael Cole and Dasha Tolstikova

MANUFACTURED IN CHINA · 10 9 8 7 6 5 4 3 2 1 · First American Edition

little mole's wish

sang-keun kim

schwartz & wade books · new york

On the day the first snow came, Little Mole was headed home by himself.

He came across a small snowball. "Hi," he said, greeting the snowball with his nose.

"Can I tell you something?" whispered Little
Mole. "I just moved here. I don't have any friends."
The snowball listened quietly.

"We're going to take the bus," said Little
Mole. "That's how we get home. It's going
to be so much fun!"

He and his friend waited patiently.

Along came Mr. Bear's bus.

"Hey, kid, you can't bring a snowball on here."

"But this is my friend," said Little Mole.

"Your friend? Snow is just snow. It'll melt."

Mr. Bear drove off.

Little Mole had a brilliant idea.

He and his friend waited patiently.

Along came Mr. Fox's bus.

"Hey, kid, you can't bring a snowball on here."

"But this is a bear," said Little Mole.

"A bear? That big lump of snow?"

Mr. Fox drove off.

Little Mole had a brilliant idea.

He and his friend waited patiently.

Night fell.

"Look, a shooting star!" exclaimed Little Mole.
"Grandma says a shooting star makes your wish
come true. I hope my wish comes true."

"Are you cold? Here, you can wear my hat."

"I'm sure the bus will be here soon."

Along came Mr. Deer's bus.

"Look at you two! You must be freezing.

Hop on. You'll catch a cold."

It was so cozy and warm on the bus.
Little Mole grew sleepy.

When Little Mole woke up, he was all alone.

"Mr. Deer, have you seen my friend?"
"I think he already got off," said
Mr. Deer kindly. "You should really hurry
home. Your family must be worried."

I didn't even get to say goodbye, Little Mole thought.

He trudged home slowly.

"There you are, little one. You're frozen solid." Grandma folded Little Mole into a warm embrace.

As always, she listened quietly as Little Mole told her about his day. "I wish I could help," she said.

That night, Little Mole couldn't fall asleep.

Where did my friend go?

The next morning, Little Mole heard Grandma calling.
"Little one, come look! You have a special visitor."